THE BIG BOO RESCUE

Adapted by Tennant Redbank

Illustrated by Judith Holmes Clarke and Larry Moore

Designed by Disney's Global Design Group

Random House 🏠 New York

HOW HAD SULLEY GOTTEN HIMSELF INTO THIS MESS?

One minute, he had been doing his job as the top Scarer for Monsters, Inc., the biggest energy supply company in Monstropolis. The next minute, he had accidentally let a human child named Boo into the monster world and uncovered a secret plot! Sulley's boss, Mr. Waternoose, and Randall Boggs, the second-best Scarer, had kidnapped Boo. They were going to use her to get an unlimited supply of scream energy!

When Waternoose had discovered Boo, he had banished Sulley and his best friend, Mike, to the Himalayas. Sulley had managed to escape and get back to Monsters, Inc. But Mike had stayed behind. He was angry with Sulley for getting them into so much trouble.

Sulley was sad to leave his best friend, but he had to rescue Boo!

In a secret lab at Monsters, Inc., Boo whimpered. She was being held prisoner in a chair, and a vacuum-like scream machine hung over her head. Randall, the mean, chameleon-like monster of her nightmares, stood next to the machine's On switch.

"Set it to ten," Randall said to Fungus, his assistant. Mr. Waternoose looked on.

The machine whirred to life. And slowly, it came closer and closer to Boo.

"RRROOAARR!"

Sulley burst through the door of the secret lab. He knocked the machine away from Boo and hurled it across the room. It pinned Mr. Waternoose and Fungus against the wall.

Then Sulley turned and gently freed Boo from the chair.

"Kitty!" Boo exclaimed in relief as Sulley picked her up.

Before Sulley could escape with Boo, he was attacked. Randall had changed his coloring to blend in with the walls around him. How could Sulley fight what he couldn't see?

Then Sulley was hit with a snowball. It was Mike! He had come back! But he was still a little mad that Sulley had left him behind in the snow.

Mike threw another snowball. It hit the invisible Randall in the face, outlining him for a moment.

And a moment was all Sulley needed. He knocked Randall out and grabbed Boo, and they all took off.

Sulley and Mike ran down the hall with Randall close behind. Mike glanced over his shoulder and saw his girlfriend, Celia, her snakes hissing at him angrily. She wanted to know what was going on! Celia grabbed Mike's legs. Sulley grabbed his arm. Neither one was letting go.

Mike tried to explain that there was a human child in Monstropolis and that Waternoose and Randall were after them. Celia didn't believe a word . . . until Boo popped up right in front of her! Celia gasped and watched wide-eyed as Mike, Sulley, and Boo raced off.

Suddenly Celia realized how she could help Mike and Sulley. "Attention, employees. Randall Boggs has just broken the all-time scare record!" she fibbed over the loudspeaker.

A mob of monsters crowded around Randall to congratulate him. "Get out of my way!" he yelled.

Meanwhile, Sulley, Mike, and Boo reached the Scare Floor. Sulley ejected a door from a door station. They grabbed on to it and were whisked away into the giant door vault of Monsters, Inc.

Rows of closet doors spread out as far as they could see. Each one was a way into a different child's room. Boo's closet door was ahead of them. They just had to get to it and return their little friend to her home.

"Look! Randall!" Mike shouted. Randall was climbing from door to door, getting closer and closer to them!

Just then, they came to a door sorter. It sent Boo's door one way and Mike, Sulley, and Boo toward a dead end. They were trapped! Or were they?

"Make Boo laugh," Sulley told Mike. If there was one thing they'd learned from Boo, it was that a child's laughter contained even more energy than a scream.

Mike bonked himself on the head. Boo laughed and the door powered up—along with every other door in the entire vault!

With thousands of doors in the door vault, Sulley knew there had to be a way to lose Randall. They could use one door to enter a room in the human world, then reenter the vault through a different door.

Sulley, Mike, and Boo went through the door they'd been riding.

That door landed them in a beach house in Hawaii. Another door dropped them in Japan. But Randall was always just a step or two behind them.

Sulley and Mike opened a door and they all jumped into a room. Randall ran through the door a moment later, but everyone had disappeared. After Randall passed by, Sulley and Mike dropped from the ceiling. They raced back the way they'd come. With a shriek, Randall followed. He launched himself at the open door. And—**SMACK!**—it slammed right in his face.

Behind the closed door, Mike chuckled. "I hope that hurt!" he said.

But nothing could keep Randall down for long. Just when Sulley thought they were safe, Randall appeared out of nowhere. He pounced on the door Sulley and Mike were riding and plucked Boo out of Sulley's arms!

Then he pulled out the pin that held the door to the track. The door, with Mike and Sulley clinging to it, dropped into the depths of the vault.

"Nice working with you!" Randall said.

"**G**et it open!" Sulley yelled.

Using all his strength, Mike managed to wrench open the door. He and Sulley crawled inside and shut the door seconds before it crashed to the ground and shattered into a million pieces.

High up in the vault, another door opened. Sulley peeked out. He spotted Boo and Randall riding a door far below. Sulley leaped from door to door, heading toward them.

His final leap brought him face to face with his enemy.

Randall opened the door and darted inside. Sulley followed.

The first thing Sulley saw was Boo standing safe and sound on the other side of the room. "Boo!" he cried in relief. But just as Sulley started toward her, Randall sprang down on him, knocking him backward and through the open door!

As he fell into the door vault, Sulley desperately reached out and caught the edge of the door. He hung dangerously over the vault.

Randall bent down and began to pry Sulley's fingers from the door.

Suddenly Randall screamed in pain. Boo was yanking on his head!

Sulley jumped back into the room and grabbed Randall. "You did it, Boo! You beat him!" Sulley said.

Boo gave Randall a big **"ROAR!"**

"She's not scared of you anymore," Sulley told Randall. "I guess you're out of a job."

With that, Sulley pitched Randall through an open door. Mike slammed it shut and dropped the door into the vault. It was the end of Randall. And it was the end of Boo's fear of Randall. Sulley had saved her. And, when it mattered most, she had overcome her fear . . . and saved him in return.

ISBN: 0-7364-1237-9

Library of Congress Control Number: 2001089026

Printed in the United States of America
October 2001

10 9 8 7 6 5 4 3 2 1

www.randomhouse.com/kids/disney